Eleven-year-old Oscar Winkle has had to put up with his little brother, Robert, for seven and a half years. Ever since Robert was born, he has been humiliating Oscar by doing things like ruining his favorite Christmas cards, spying on him while he tries on his new underwear, and even dumping a whole box of live spiders on his bedroom floor!

In Barbara Park's latest hilarious escapade, *Operation: Dump the Chump,* Oscar reveals a secret plan to get rid of Robert for a whole summer that will have young readers laughing out loud.

# OPERATION: Dump the Chump

## by BARBARA PARK

Alfred A. Knopf · New York

To Mom and Dad
*Thank You*

This is a Borzoi Book published by Alfred A. Knopf, Inc.

Text Copyright © 1982 by Barbara Park
Cover illustration Copyright © 1982 by Rob Sauber
All rights reserved under International and Pan-American
Copyright Conventions. Published in the United States by
Alfred A. Knopf, Inc., New York, and simultaneously in
Canada by Random House of Canada Limited, Toronto.
Distributed by Random House, Inc., New York.
Manufactured in the United States of America
10  9  8  7  6  5  4  3  2  1

Library of Congress Cataloging in Publication Data
Park, Barbara. Operation dump the chump.
Summary: Eleven-year-old Oscar devises an elaborate
plan to get rid of his pesky little brother.
[1. Brothers and sisters—Fiction]  I. Title.
PZ7.P21970p  1981  [Fic]      81-8147
ISBN 0-394-94976-5 (lib. bdg.)   AACR2
ISBN 0-394-84976-0

# OPERATION:
# Dump
# the Chump

# Meet the Chump

I've never really liked my brother. Never. And it's silly to pretend I do.

I keep trying to explain this to my mother, but she doesn't seem to be getting the message. She's always saying stuff like, "Oh, you don't really mean that, Oscar. Deep down inside, you know you love him."

She's wrong. Deep down inside, I know the kid's a creep.

I knew he was going to be a creep the first day my mother brought him home from the hospital. I was almost four years old when he was born, so I can remember exactly what happened.

I was watching my favorite cartoon show when my mother walked through the front door. She was carrying a big bundle of blue blankets.

Dad was right behind her with the suitcases. He didn't say hello or anything. He just dropped the suitcases and started rushing around trying to get his camera equipment down from the hall closet.

My mother walked into the living room and stood between me and the television. She was grinning from ear to ear.

"I've got someone in this blanket who would love to meet you," she said.

I started to peek around her skirt to see the TV, but my father came in and unplugged the set. The cartoon faded and the screen went blank.

"I need this outlet for my movie light," he announced, busily setting up his equipment.

Mom walked over to the couch and sat down next to me. She pulled one of the blankets off the baby's head.

"Oscar," she said, "I'd like you to meet your new baby brother, Robert. Can you say hi?"

What an insulting question! Of course I could say hi! I had been saying hi for years. The thing was, I didn't *want* to say hi.

"That's silly," I said to my mother. "He's just a baby."

"I know," she said, "but wouldn't it be nice if you said hi and gave him a little kiss?"

Now she wanted me to give him a kiss! I didn't even know this kid!

I took a quick peek under the blankets. His face was all puffy and he didn't have much hair. I would have rather kissed a snake.

Suddenly, the light to the movie camera flashed in my eyes. It was so bright I was almost blinded.

"Get ready!" shouted my father. "Okay ... Action!"

Before I knew what was happening, my mother had put the baby on my lap.

"Wave, Oscar! Wave!" she ordered.

I waved.

"Okay," said my father. "Now lean down and give baby Robert a nice big kiss!"

Oh no! I thought. This is it! They're really going to make me kiss him!

I looked down at Robert. But something about him looked different. His face had turned red and he was getting a real silly grin on his face. Suddenly, he began making all these disgusting grunting noises.

It didn't take long to figure out what he was doing. Yuck! I just had to get him off my lap!

Quickly, I stood up. And when I did, Robert landed on the floor.

He wasn't hurt or anything. How could he be hurt with all those blankets around him? But he started to scream his head off anyway.

The next thing I knew, my father had grabbed me by the arm and was putting me in my room. I couldn't believe it! Robert goes to the bathroom on my lap, and I'm the one who gets punished! Right then and there, I knew the kid was going to be a creep.

So far I've been right about Robert. He's almost eight now, and he's even creepier than ever.

I used to hope that when he started school, he would settle down. But it hasn't worked out that way at all. I was a lot better off before Robert ever learned how to read and write.

Last Christmas was the perfect example. For

the first time ever, my mother said I could choose my own Christmas cards to send to my friends. I was really excited about it. My mom even gave me five dollars and told me to go to the store and pick out any kind I wanted. She said she would trust my judgment.

When I got to the store it didn't take long to spot the exact cards I wanted to buy. They had this funny Santa standing there with an elf sitting on his head. The Santa was saying, "MERRY CHRISTMAS, _____!" You were supposed to fill in the blank space with the name of the person you were sending it to.

I bought them and hurried home to show my mother.

"I'm home!" I shouted excitedly as I ran in the door. "Wait till you see the cards I picked out!"

"I just got in the tub!" yelled my mother. "Leave them on the table and I'll look at them when I get out."

I put my new box of cards on the kitchen table and went into the family room to watch TV.

Later, when I heard my mother come out of

the bathroom, I rushed to the kitchen to get them. But the cards were gone.

It didn't take long to find them, though. All I had to do was look in Robert's room. He had taken all my cards and written "POOPOO HED" in the spaces where the names were supposed to go. Every single card had Santa standing there saying, "MERRY CHRISTMAS, POOPOO HED!"

I was so mad I started to cry.

I ran into the bedroom to show my mother.

"Look what that little creep wrote all over my new cards!" I screamed.

My mother took the cards and looked them over. "Merry Christmas, Poopoo Hed," she read out loud.

She kept her head bent down for several seconds. I think she was trying to keep herself from laughing. Finally, she looked up.

"He spelled 'head' wrong," she said.

I couldn't believe it! My jerky brother ruined my Christmas cards, and all my mother could do was correct his spelling!

"Geez, Mother!" I yelled. "This isn't a spelling bee! Aren't you going to do something?"

My mother called Robert into her room. (He had been hiding in his closet.) She told him he would have to use his own money to buy me a new box of cards. Big deal. Some punishment. If you ask me, I think she should have sent him to his room and made him miss Christmas.

Of course Christmas isn't the only holiday that Robert has ruined for me. Over the past few years he has also managed to ruin Easter, Halloween, Thanksgiving, Valentine's Day, the Fourth of July, and my birthday. In fact, until this year, I thought that Robert had ruined every single "fun" day possible. But I was wrong. This year he even ruined my school field trip.

It happened a couple of months ago. Our class was going to visit the Museum of Natural History in the city. And I couldn't wait to go. I'd go anywhere to get out of doing schoolwork.

A week before the trip my teacher sent a note home asking parents to pack their kids a sack lunch. I wish she hadn't done that. That note turned out to be the start of my problem.

My mother must think that going on a field trip turns me into a real pig. You should have seen the giant lunch she packed. It wouldn't even fit into a regular lunch bag, so she had to pack it in a big brown grocery sack!

I saw it sitting on the counter that morning when I came to breakfast. I tried to scrunch it down to make it look smaller. But no matter what I did, it still looked like a grocery sack.

Then, as if that wasn't bad enough, while I was eating my cereal, my mother took a big fat marking pen and wrote OSCAR T. WINKLE on the front of the bag. I guess she was afraid someone would try to steal all my "goodies."

Well, I hate to tell her, but most kids would rather starve than steal a lunch sack that looked as dumb as mine did.

After my mother finished making my lunch look ridiculous, Robert came walking into the kitchen. He took one look at that dumb sack sitting there and fell right down on the floor laughing. He couldn't stop.

Finally, he pointed to the sack and read it out loud.

"Oscar T. Winkle," he said. "Gee, I never noticed that before."

"Noticed what, creep-head?" I asked.

"Your middle initial turns Winkle into Twinkle! Twinkle. That's kind of a cute little name, don't you think, Twink?"

Then the jerky kid fell right out of his chair laughing again. "Wait till your friends see it, Twinkie" he roared. "They'll love it!"

My mother sent him to his room. I think she was mad because he was making fun of her sack. But it was too late. The damage had already been done.

Robert had made me so nervous about my sack that at lunchtime I went off in a corner and ate by myself. I hate to eat alone. Every time someone walks by, they think you're either weird or that you smell bad. It's humiliating.

*Humiliate.* That's the perfect word for what Robert does. He humiliates me. If you don't know what it means, I'll give you an example. Humiliated is how you feel when your brother takes your jockstrap to school for Show and Tell. I know. Robert's done it.

As a matter of fact, Robert has done almost every creepy thing you can think of. But a guy like me can only take so much. After that, he has to take things into his own hands. And that's just what I did when I created my plan to get rid of Robert.

I called it, Operation: Dump the Chump.

# Step Number One

We live in one of those neighborhoods that you see on television commercials. You know, the kind with lots of shady oak trees and big white houses with screened-in porches. I guess it's a nice place to live, but I'm not sure. When you have to live with Robert, no place seems very nice.

At the corner of the street, about eight houses down from us, live the Hensons. Mr. Henson is about eighty years old, but he's still in pretty good shape. And he really likes kids. When Robert and I were younger, we would go down to the Hensons' and Mr. Henson would give us rides in his wheelbarrow.

He laughs a lot. And sometimes when he smiles, he doesn't have all his false teeth in, and you can see his gums. You don't really want to look at them, but you have to.

There is only one thing about Mr. Henson that really bothers me. I don't want to say anything mean about such a nice man, but Mr. Henson has a bunch of wiry gray hairs growing out of his ears. I think I'd like him a whole lot better if he would clip them off.

Mrs. Henson looks a little younger than Mr. Henson. It's hard to tell, but I figure she's only about seventy-five. Maybe she just seems younger because she still wears shorts a lot. Her knees are real saggy, but Mrs. Henson just jokes about them.

It seems like nothing ever bothers Mrs. Henson. I guess that's why she's never gotten Mr. Henson to clip his ear hairs.

You can always get Mrs. Henson to pet your gerbils. She'll touch anything. One time, I actually saw Mrs. Henson pick up a dead bird with her bare hands and dump it in her trash can. She didn't even have gloves on!

Nope. Nothing bothers Mrs. Henson at all. Not even Robert.

The Hensons were going to play a very big part in Operation: Dump the Chump. They didn't know it, of course. This plan was absolutely Top Secret. But without the help of Mr. and Mrs. Henson, there would have been no plan at all. So I had to be very careful.

The first step of Operation: Dump the Chump was extremely important. I had to wait until just the right moment to begin. Meanwhile, I spent my free time planning everything out very carefully.

My patience finally paid off. It was the second Saturday in May. The sun was shining, and I was pretty sure Mr. Henson would be outside working in his garden. Robert was at baseball practice and would not be home for at least an hour and a half. The timing was perfect!

"I'm going out for a while, Mom," I shouted as I ran out the screen door. I heard her shout something back, so I went back in.

"What did you say?" I yelled.

"I asked you where you were going," she said.

"Around," I answered as I started out the door again.

"Around where?" shouted my mother.

I just hate it when she asks dumb questions

like that! How am I supposed to know "around where"? And even if I do, why does *she* always have to know, too? Just once, I wish my mom would shout, "I don't care where you go or what you do, Oscar. It's none of my business. Just have fun and come home whenever you feel like it." But I know it will never happen.

"Did you hear the question, Oscar?" my mother shouted again. "Around where?"

"I'm not sure where," I yelled back. "Just around outside somewhere, I guess."

This answer still didn't tell her where I would be, but for some reason it seemed to satisfy her.

"Okay, honey," she said. "Have a good time."

Mothers are very strange.

As soon as I left the house, I headed right for the Hensons'. Sure enough, when I got there, Mr. Henson was out front weeding his garden just as I thought.

"Hi, Mr. Henson," I called, walking over to him.

He looked up and smiled. He didn't have his teeth in.

"Why, hello there, young fella," he said.

Mr. Henson always calls me young fella. I think it's probably because he just can't stand the name Oscar. One time he tried calling me Osc. But it sounded more like Ox. He must have thought so, too. Because he's been calling me young fella ever since.

"What'cha up to, today?" he asked.

"Oh, not much Mr. Henson," I answered. "Just kind of hanging around, I guess."

"Where's that little brother of yours? he asked.

This was just the question I was waiting for! I was almost positive he would ask it, and I was right! Whenever I'm alone, Mr. Henson always asks me where dumb Robert is. Step Number One of Operation: Dump the Chump was about to begin.

"Well, the thing is, Mr. Henson," I began, "I would like to tell you where Robert is, but I'm not allowed. My parents made me promise not to talk about it."

Mr. Henson looked puzzled for a minute. Then he said, "Well okay, young fella, then why don't we talk about the World Series. Who do you think will make it this year?"

I couldn't believe it! What the heck was wrong with him? I'm standing there with a giant secret, and he doesn't even try to get it out of me! I figured he'd be begging me to tell him. It just goes to show you. You can never count on grownups to do what they're supposed to do. Mr. Henson was really messing up Step Number One. I just *had* to get him to ask me about Robert.

"Gee, Mr. Henson," I continued, "I don't really know a whole lot about the teams this year. It's too bad Robert isn't here. Now, *there's* a kid who knows baseball. Good old Robert. Yup, too bad *he's* not here. Poor, good old Robert."

Well, you're not going to believe this, but do you know what Mr. Henson said then? He said, "Oh well, I guess it's too early to talk about the World Series, anyway."

I just couldn't stand it!

"Mr. Henson!" I blurted out. "Don't you even *care* what happens to my poor brother, Robert? What's wrong with you, anyway? Robert's always liked *you*, Mr. Henson. And I've liked you, too. And now, when poor Robert's in real trouble, you act like you don't even care! Boy, Mr. Henson, am I ever disappointed in you!"

I didn't mean to say all that stuff, honest. It's just that when I have a plan and it starts going wrong, I get upset. And, when I'm upset, I say stuff I don't mean to say. Mr. Henson looked upset, too.

"Whoa, now! Hold on there, young fella," he said. "Just simmer down a minute and tell old Mr. Henson what's going on here. Has something happened to Robert? Something you think I should know about?"

Ah, now that was more like it!

"Well okay, Mr. Henson," I said finally. "If you're going to keep bugging me about my secret, I guess I'll have to tell you." (This is what I had planned to say if everything had gone right. So I decided to say it anyway.)

"See the thing is, Mr. Henson," I began, "last night my father came home from work with some really terrible news."

"What kind of news?" he asked immediately. Boy! Was he ever curious now!

"The worst," I answered sadly. "My poor father lost his job yesterday."

"Oh no," said Mr. Henson. "What happened?"

"Well," I explained, "My dad's boss told him

that he had been clowning around in the office too much. And since he was making everyone laugh, no one could get their work done. So his boss fired him. Just like that, Mr. Henson. That mean man fired my father!"

Mr. Henson walked over to his front porch and sat down on the steps. Now he really looked upset.

"Oh dear," he said finally. "This whole thing is just terrible. It really is." Then he paused a minute and looked up. "But I'm afraid I still don't understand what it has to do with Robert," he said.

"I was just getting to that part," I replied. "You see, after my father finished telling us the bad news, he went up to his room to cry his eyes out or something. And after he was gone, my mother told Robert and me that she didn't think there was going to be enough money to feed all four of us for a while."

"Oh my goodness," said Mr. Henson.

"Yeah, 'Oh my goodness' is right," I said. "I knew what my mother was hinting at, Mr. Henson. She wanted to ask one of us to move out, but she didn't have the heart to say it. So I did her a favor."

"What do you mean, young fella?" he asked. "What kind of favor?"

"I volunteered to find another place to live for a while," I said proudly. "But unfortunately, my mother said no."

"Why did she say no?" he asked. "I thought you said that's what she wanted."

"She did, Mr. Henson," I answered. "But the trouble is I hardly eat enough to keep a bird alive. See how skinny my wrists are?"

I held out my wrists so he could look at them.

Then I continued. "My mother said that it probably wouldn't do much good for me to move out. She said if a family wants to cut down on their food bills, it's the pig of the family that has to go. And in our family, Mr. Henson, the piggo is Robert. We'd put him on a diet, but my mother says it might stunt his growth."

Mr. Henson didn't answer. He stood up and began walking around. The whole time he was walking, he kept shaking his head and mumbling to himself. Boy, was he taking this thing hard!

I got up and walked over to his garden.

"Wow, Mr. Henson!" I exclaimed. "Look at all these vegetables you've planted! I bet you've planted enough vegetables to feed a whole army of kids! Wow! I'm going to have to bring Robert over here and let him see your garden. Boy, does that kid ever love home-grown vegetables!"

Mr. Henson smiled. But his smile didn't last long. After a couple of minutes he wandered back over to the porch and sat down again. He looked very puzzled.

"Don't you think your father will be able to get another job soon?" he asked. "He works at the bank, doesn't he? Surely there must be other banking jobs available. Or how about your mother? Maybe your mother can go to work for a while to help out."

To tell you the truth, even though I thought I had planned Step Number One very carefully, I didn't expect Mr. Henson to ask all those questions. And I wasn't prepared for them at all. So the only thing I could do was to make up the answers as I went along.

"Well . . . ah . . ." I stuttered, "see . . . the thing is

. . . my father said that his boss called most of the other banks in town and told them not to hire him because he was such a troublemaker. And . . . hmmm . . . as for my mother . . . well, of course she would work if she could, but unfortunately, she never learned how." (Boy, if my mother could have heard that one, she would have killed me!)

"Well, what about savings?" questioned Mr. Henson. "Didn't your father have any savings for an emergency? Or relatives? Couldn't he borrow money from his family?"

Geez! Where in the world was he getting all these questions? I started to panic. And when I did, my answers got even dumber.

"Well . . . ah . . . my father used to have some savings, Mr. Henson, but he gave it all to my grandfather so he could have an operation to remove the hair from his ears. He couldn't hear very well without the operation. I guess you know how annoying hair in the old ears can be. . . ."

Mr. Henson just stared at me. I wasn't sure if he believed me or not, but I had to keep going.

"And . . . ah . . . well . . . as for my father's

relatives . . . well, you probably won't believe this, Mr. Henson, but my father is the only one in his family who has ever had a job. He has two brothers, but they're both bums. I think they live out on the desert somewhere."

"Oh my," said Mr. Henson, when I had finished. This is just awful, young fella. Your poor, poor family."

"Yeah, poor, poor us, all right," I said. "And especially poor, poor Robert. He's so young to be going off on his own. I sure hope my parents find him a good home. It's too bad we don't know anyone who would like to have a wonderful little kid like Robert come and stay with them for a while."

I waited for a minute to see if Mr. Henson had any more questions. He didn't. So I turned and started for home.

"Thanks for listening, Mr. Henson," I said as I walked away. "I'd better be getting home now. My poor mother's probably wondering where I am. She's going to need me to help her out a lot more, now that Robert's not going to be around."

I took a few steps toward my house, and then

stopped. "Poor, poor little Robert," I said loud enough for Mr. Henson to hear. "What a brave little soldier he is."

"Oh, by the way, Mr. Henson," I added, looking up. "Please, please don't say anything about this to *anyone*, especially not to Robert. It makes all of us very, very sad to talk about it. And I know you wouldn't want to do anything to make things worse. Besides, Mr. Henson, my parents would *kill* me if they knew I had told you all our problems."

"Don't worry about me, young fella," said Mr. Henson. "I won't say a word." Then he turned to go inside.

I headed for home. The first step of Operation: Dump the Chump was complete. And, if you asked me, it had gone very, very well!

# Step Number Two

After I left the Hensons' house I went right home to get ready for Step Number Two. I was pretty excited about how well things were going, but I didn't want to rush into the second step of my plan too quickly. If I did, I knew I could blow the whole thing. I needed time to think.

As soon as I walked in the door, my mother asked, "Home so soon, Oscar? What happened?"

"Nothing to do," I answered, trying to sound normal. "I think I'll just go up to my room for a while."

"Why?" she asked. "Don't you feel well?"

Now, this is another thing that really kills me about my mother. For some reason she seems to think that as long as I'm outside, I'm healthy. But as soon as I want to come inside, I'm sick. It just doesn't make sense. If being inside means you're sick, then my mother must be sick all the time.

"I feel fine, Mother," I answered sharply, "just fine."

Then I ran up to my room and locked the door. Once it was locked, I checked the closet and the windows to make sure no one was spying on me. Checking the windows may sound like a strange thing to do, since my room is on the second floor. But with a sneak like Robert around, you can't be too careful.

One time, about a year ago, my mother went out shopping to buy me some new underwear. When she came home, she asked me to go up to my room and try it on. She wanted to make sure it was the right size.

I really didn't want to do it, but once when she bought me underwear, the leg holes were too big. And when I wore them to school, Joanne Reilly told the whole gym class that every time I climbed the rope she could look right up my shorts and see "everything." So since then, I decided that if my mother wanted me to try on new underwear, I'd do it.

Anyway, that day while I was in my room trying on this underwear, I caught a glimpse of myself in the mirror. And to tell you the truth, I really looked pretty good.

I got the chair from my desk and carried it back over to my dresser. Then, I stood up on the chair so I could get a better look at myself.

Hmmm, I thought. The old leg muscles aren't too bad either. I started flexing. That's when the laughter started. It was coming from outside my window. I looked over, and there, standing on a ladder staring right into my bedroom was dumb, jerk-o Robert!

"Va-va-va-voom!" he shouted, roaring at the top of his lungs. Then he whistled at me.

I was so mad at Robert I must have gone crazy for a minute. The next thing I knew, I was running down the stairs and right out the front door into the yard.

I caught Robert just as he was on the third step of the ladder. I wasted no time pulling him the rest of the way down. Then I clobbered him as hard as I could.

Robert screamed so loud that Mr. and Mrs. Farley from next door came running out of their house to see what was going on. That's when I realized that I was still in my underwear.

I was so embarrassed, I didn't know what to do. And neither did the Farleys. So we all just stood there staring at each other.

Finally I just kind of waved at them and said, "Hi there, Mr. and Mrs. Farley. How do you like my new underwear?"

Mrs. Farley didn't answer. She just shook her head real disgustedly and walked back to her house. But Mr. Farley took a few steps in my direction and put his hands on his hips. "For heaven's sake, Oscar," he said. "Don't you think you're rather old to be running around the neighborhood in your panties?"

Panties! The guy actually called my underwear panties! I've never really forgiven Mr. Farley for that.

Anyway, after that, I turned around and went back inside. Robert was in the kitchen crying. I guess I must have clobbered him harder than I thought. My mother was waiting for me in the hallway.

Wow! I thought. I'm really going to get it now.

But my mother surprised me. I guess when she saw how ridiculous I looked standing there in my underwear, she figured I had already been through enough. Instead of yelling, she walked over to me, snapped the elastic waistband of my new underpants, and said, "Nice fit, Oscar. You're really becoming quite a snappy dresser."

Well, the whole point of this story is that when you have a brother like Robert, you've got to be very careful. And that's why I checked the closet and the windows before I pulled out the notebook containing my secret plans for Operation: Dump the Chump.

Then I sat down on my bed and opened the notebook to page one. I took a pencil and made a check mark beside Step Number One, which said, "Tell Hensons that Robert needs a home." Then, I looked over the rest of the steps to my plan. There were eight in all:

### Operation: Dump the Chump

Step Number One:  Tell Hensons that Robert needs a home.

Step Number Two:  Tell parents that Hensons need a boy.

Step Number Three: Put fake ad in paper
from Hensons.

Step Number Four: Show fake ad to
parents.

Step Number Five: Put fake ad in paper
from parents.

Step Number Six: Show fake ad to Hensons.

Step Number Seven: Write fake letter to
Hensons.

Step Number Eight: Write fake letter to
parents.

I laughed with excitement as I read my plans
over and over again. "Oscar old boy, you're a
genius—a real genius!" I said out loud.

I re-read Step Number Two: "Tell parents that
Hensons need a boy."

This wasn't going to be quite as easy as the
first step had been. I knew that if she wanted to,
my mother could ask a thousand more questions than Mr. Henson. This time I had to be
ready for anything.

I got right to work. First I wrote down everything I planned to say. Next I made a list of all

the dumb questions I thought my mother might ask. Then I studied it carefully.

I guess I must have been working at it longer than I thought, because before I knew it, I heard her calling me for lunch. I took a deep breath. I was ready.

"Where's Robert?" I asked as I sat down to eat my lunch all alone.

"Oh, he called and asked if he could eat over at the Bradfords'," said my mother.

Perfect! Robert wouldn't be back for a while, and I had my mother all to myself.

I sat there, not saying a word as I ate my sandwich. Pretty soon my mother said, "You're awfully quiet, Oscar. Is something the matter? Are you upset?"

I knew it! I *knew* she would ask me that! I had even *planned* on it. She just can't stand it when I'm quiet. According to my mother, if you come inside, you're sick, and if you don't feel like talking, you're upset.

"Come on, tell me what's bothering you," she said again.

"Oh, I don't know," I said, sounding *really*

unhappy. "I was just sitting here thinking about poor Mrs. Henson." (Geez, was I ever good at this! I should be an actor!)

"You mean Mrs. Henson, down the street?" she asked. "Did something happen to her?"

"Well, not exactly," I said slowly. "It's just that she was telling me about some problems she's been having lately."

"Problems? What kind of problems?" asked my mother.

"Well, it's just that Mr. Henson is getting pretty old now. And Mrs. Henson says he's not as strong as he used to be. She told me that sometimes he needs help getting around," I answered.

"Did Mr. Henson fall and break something?" she asked. "Is he ill? Are you saying that he can't walk?"

"No, Mom," I answered. "Mr. Henson didn't fall down or anything. It just seems that his bones aren't as strong as they used to be, and he can't get around very well. That's why I feel so sorry for Mrs. Henson. She has to do almost everything all by herself. And she told me how tired she's been getting lately, that's all."

My mother kept up with more questions. "When did you talk to Mrs. Henson about this, Oscar?" she asked. "Why did she tell you all those things? Was she upset or something?"

"Okay, okay," I answered. "I guess I might as well tell you the whole story. I saw Mrs. Henson outside this morning. She looked real sad, like she had been crying or something, so I stopped and asked her if something was wrong. That's when she told me all this stuff about her husband. All she kept saying was how tired she was and how nice it would be if they had a boy around the house to help out with the chores. But Mrs. Henson said that they just don't have enough money to hire anyone."

"That's funny," said my mother right away. "They had enough money to fly to Hawaii for Christmas last year. They can't be *that* poor."

Oh no! I could have kicked myself. I had forgotten all about the Hensons' trip to Hawaii! I felt myself beginning to panic again.

"Ah . . . yeah . . . well," I stuttered, "ah . . . Mrs. Henson told me that when they were in Hawaii a hula girl broke into their room and stole all their money. (It sounded dumb, but it was better than nothing.) "And it's really a shame," I continued quickly. "Because Mrs. Henson said it was all the savings they had. It's lucky that they had already bought their plane tickets for home. Otherwise they probably would have had to spend the rest of their lives as beach bums."

My mother just stood there looking at me for a minute. I had a feeling she didn't buy the whole story. So I hurried to get on to another subject.

"Anyway," I said quickly, "poor Mrs. Henson really does need help, Mom. Before I left today, she told me that she didn't think her poor old back could hold up much longer. Especially if she has to keep dragging Mr. Henson around the house all night."

"Dragging? What do you mean, dragging?" my mother asked.

"Oh, I forgot to tell you. Mrs. Henson told me that sometimes at night, when Mr. Henson is especially tired out, she has to drag him wherever he wants to go. Sometimes she drags him to dinner and then later she drags him upstairs to bed. It really must be hard on her."

"Oh no!" said my mother. (I knew that "dragging" stuff would get to her.) "This is just terrible, Oscar!" Then she paused for a second. "Hmm," she continued with a puzzled look on her face. "But if what you're saying is true, I wonder what Mr. Henson was doing outside working in his garden this morning. I saw him when I took Robert to baseball practice."

This was one question I was ready for.

"Well, Mrs. Henson told me that he has good days and bad days," I answered. "She was telling me that one day last week, Mr. Henson thought he felt well enough to work in his garden. But when he bent over and started to weed, he got so tired he flopped over and took a nap right smack on his vegetables. She said he squished a whole row of squash."

My mother looked very confused and worried. But she didn't ask any more questions. She just stood there shaking her head the same way Mr. Henson had done.

Meanwhile, I finished the rest of my lunch and got up to leave. The second step of Operation: Dump the Chump was almost completed. Only one more thing needed to be said.

As I was walking away, I mumbled something to myself.

"What did you say, honey?" asked my mother. She really can't stand it when somebody mumbles around her.

"Oh nothing," I answered. "It's just that I was thinking about how much Robert has always liked those Hensons. And it's funny, but the Hensons must really like him too. Do you know what Mrs. Henson said when I was leaving today?"

"No, what?" asked my mother, concerned.

"She said, 'Oscar, please don't tell anyone what I've just told you. I don't want anyone worrying about us. And most of all, please don't tell your little brother, Robert. We'd really hate to upset him with news like this. That Robert's always such a happy little boy. He must be such a joy to your parents.' That's what she said, Mom. She called Robert a joy."

My mother didn't say anything. But I could tell she was thinking.

"Well, I guess I'll go back outside for a while," I said. "Maybe I'll run down to the Hensons' and see if they need any help."

Quickly, I left the kitchen and went out the back door. I ran down the street and when I got far enough away from the house, I jumped into the air and shouted, "*Yeeehaaa!*" Two steps down and six to go. Then it's good-bye Robert!

# Step Number Three

The next day was Sunday. And as everyone knows, Sunday is the most boring day of the week. I don't know what makes it so different from Saturday, but somehow it never turns out to be as much fun.

My mother always fixes a special big breakfast on Sunday morning. I'm not really sure why she does this, but it seems to make her happy, so I always eat it whether I'm hungry or not.

A lot of people I know get all dressed up and go to church on Sunday. We tried that for a while, but it just didn't seem to work out.

My mother had signed us up for Sunday school at the church down the street. She told us we would have a lot of fun and learn about the Bible. She was wrong. All I really learned was that I stink at art.

Every week in Sunday school we did the same thing. First our teacher would pass out Bible pictures for us to color. Then she would put this box of old broken crayons on the table and tell us to "get busy." Most of the crayons were so little, you couldn't get a good grip on them and your picture ended up looking like scribble.

When you were finished coloring, the teacher always had an art project for you to work on. The first week we had to make a little church out of a small milk carton. Mine didn't turn out very well. My little church ended up looking like a little barn. When the teacher saw it she got this real disgusted look on her face. She asked me if I was trying to be funny. She said I shouldn't be making a joke out of "God's house." I didn't say anything. I decided that I would rather let her think I was a smart-aleck than to admit it was the best I could do. After that I wasn't too excited about going back to Sunday school.

Robert didn't seem to like it any better than I did. It's probably the only thing we've ever agreed on in our whole lives. He's the one who got us kicked out.

One Sunday we were supposed to color a picture of baby Jesus with a halo around his head. The class had just started working on it, when all of a sudden I saw the teacher grab Robert's picture away from him and put it in the trash. Then she took away his crayons and made him sit at the table all by himself.

When the teacher wasn't looking, I went over and got Robert's crumpled picture out of the trash can to see what he had done. Robert had drawn a big black mustache on the baby's face. I have to admit, it really did look pretty funny. I wonder if God has a sense of humor. I figure he probably does. Sometimes I think he made Robert as a joke.

Anyway, our teacher didn't let Robert work on the project that week. We were making halos, and I guess she figured that Robert didn't deserve one. When my mother came to pick us up that morning I heard the teacher tell her that she didn't think Robert should come back unless he could behave better.

My mother must have been very embarrassed. She yelled at Robert for a long time and then told us that we couldn't go back to Sunday school until we got a little bit older. I think my mother thought that she was punishing us. What she doesn't know won't hurt her.

On Sunday, Robert seems to get on my nerves more than any other day of the week. He does it on purpose. Usually he starts right after break-fast.

As soon as I get up from the breakfast table, I go up to my room to get dressed. Robert sits outside my door and pretends he can see me un-dressing through the keyhole. I know he can't, but just to be sure, I always tape a piece of paper over the hole. Just to show you what a jerk Robert is, every week he still sits there and pretends he sees me changing clothes. He whis-tles and everything. What an idiot.

After I'm dressed, I usually hang around the house for a while, telling my mother that there's nothing to do. Finally she gets mad and makes me go outside.

As soon as I'm outside, Robert does the same dumb thing. Every single Sunday he spies on me. Stupid, right? Well, that's Robert for you—just plain stupid.

Robert has got to be the worst spy in the whole world. He always tries to hide behind these real skinny little trees. You can see him perfectly! What a jerk.

Finally, I just couldn't stand it any more, so I decided to teach him a lesson.

After breakfast I went outside as usual and sat down on the porch steps. Pretty soon I heard Robert crawling through the bushes on the side of the house. He was about as quiet as a bulldozer. Some spy!

Anyway, I just sat there on the step for a while, pretending I didn't know he was in the bushes spying on me. Then, after a few more minutes, I got up and started walking around the yard. I acted like I was looking for something. I looked all around my mother's flower beds and then around some of the trees. Then I walked over to the bushes where Robert was hiding. Boy, was he ever being quiet.

"Hmm," I said, still pretending I had lost something. "I wonder where that darn thing went?"

Robert wasn't moving a muscle. He was quiet as a mouse.

That's when I started spitting. I stood right there in front of the bushes and spit like I had never spit before.

Robert came flying out!

"You dummy!" he shouted. "I'm telling Mom!" Then he rushed into the house.

Pretty soon my mother came out. Robert was right behind her, "Oscar, what's this I hear about you spitting on your brother? That's the most disgusting thing I've ever heard!" she said. I've never seen her so mad!

"I didn't spit on him," I said.

That's when Robert came over to me and showed me his shirt. There were two little blobs of spit on the shoulder.

"What do you call that, then?" he asked. He was really burned up!

"You shouldn't drool on yourself like that, Robert," I said. I thought this was a pretty funny thing to say. Unfortunately, my mother didn't.

"I didn't mean to spit on him," I insisted. "I was just watering the bushes! How was I supposed to know he was in there spying on me? If you want to yell at someone, yell at *him* for spying!

If he wasn't hiding out in the bushes, he would never have gotten spit on!"

I guess my mother wasn't in the mood to decide who was right or wrong, because we both got sent to our rooms.

But, I've got to admit, seeing Robert's shirt with those two little blobs of spit on it was worth being punished.

Besides, being in my room gave me a lot of time alone to work on the third step of Operation: Dump the Chump. I took out my secret notebook and checked it carefully. It said, "Step Number Three: Put fake ad in paper from Hensons." I knew this wasn't going to be easy. I had never written an ad before. I definitely needed help.

I went downstairs and asked my mother if I could read the Sunday paper while I was up in my room being punished. I'm sure she wondered why I wanted it—I had *never* read the paper before, not in my entire life—but she let me have it without a lot of questions.

The first thing I did was open it up to the classified ads section. Classified ads are ads that people write when they want or need something special—for instance, if you want to hire someone for a special job, or if you want to sell something you don't want anymore.

As I studied the ads, I noticed that most of them were only a couple of lines long. Hmmm, I thought, maybe this isn't going to be that difficult after all. Then, at the bottom of the page I found a telephone number to call if you wanted to put an ad in the paper. All you had to do was pick up the phone! I was really getting excited.

I went over to my desk and began to write a few samples of the ad I wanted. I worked for quite some time, but finally I had it! It went like this:

WANTED: Nice young boy to live
with old couple. Call 561-3447.

I read it over and over again. I had to admit, it sounded awfully good. As a matter of fact, it sounded almost as if the Hensons had actually written it themselves!

The very next morning I called the paper. I

told the lady on the phone that I wanted to place an ad in Sunday's paper. It was so simple I could hardly believe it! All I had to do was read her my ad.

She told me that my ad would probably go in the "Personal" section of the ads. I told her she could put it wherever she wanted to, just as long as it was in next Sunday's paper.

Before she hung up, the newspaper lady asked me how I wanted to pay for the ad.

"How much is it?" I asked.

"Three dollars," she answered. "If you like, you can come to our business office and pay for it. Or, if you prefer, we can send you a bill."

"A bill?" I gasped. "Oh no! Don't send me a bill! I'm too young for bills!" (If my mother ever saw a newspaper bill addressed to me, my whole plan would be ruined!) "I'll just ride my bike to your office after school," I said.

The lady laughed, but then she told me where the office was located. It was right across the street from the post office. I knew I would have no trouble finding it.

After I hung up, I went to my bank and stuffed

three dollars into my jeans. I told my mother I would be late getting home from school. I said I was working on a big project.

It wasn't a lie either. Operation: Dump the Chump was the biggest project of my life.

# Step Number Four

The week that followed seemed to drag on forever. I thought Sunday would never come. All I could think about was my ad being in the Sunday paper and how it would look. Every few days I pulled out my notebook and re-read the fourth step of my plan: "Show fake ad to parents."

This was going to be a very important part of my operation. I had to make my parents believe that the ad in the paper had been written by the Hensons. So in my mind I memorized all the things I might need to say to convince them. But as it turned out, it was easier than I thought.

When Sunday finally came, I went down to breakfast the same as usual. And of course, Robert was already at the table, gulping down his juice like a slob.

"Good morning, Mom and Dad," I said, sounding more cheerful than I'd meant to sound.

They both smiled.

"Good morning, dribble-puss," I mumbled to Robert.

"Don't start," said my father. He gave me a look like he always does when he thinks a fight is about to break out.

My mother had just started making the pancakes, so breakfast was going a little slow. It was very hard for me to sit there for so long trying to act normal. Inside I was so nervous about my ad that I could hardly stand it.

Robert started talking about how good his baseball team was doing. I wouldn't have minded this quite so much if he hadn't kept saying how glad he was that he hadn't been placed on a stink-o team like mine.

"Will someone please tell Robert to shut up?" I asked nicely. But then I decided to do it myself.

"If anyone knows anything about being stink-o, it's you Robert. You're so stink-o, I can smell you from here."

My father squinted his eyes at me and rustled his paper. But he didn't yell. He's not very good at yelling in the morning. He's too interested in his paper. At our house my mother is in charge of all the morning yelling.

"If I hear one more 'stink-o' " she said, "both of you are going to leave the table without breakfast."

I know my mother well enough to know that she meant what she said. So I decided to shut up. Robert wasn't as smart.

After a couple of minutes I heard him whisper "stink-o" one more time. I think he only did it to see if my mother meant business. She did. Robert left the table immediately.

After the pancakes were served, I ate my breakfast in silence. The whole time I was eating I watched my father as he read the paper. My heart was pounding. I knew that my ad was somewhere in that very paper.

After I finished eating I left the table and casually asked my father if I could take the paper up to my room to read.

"What's all this sudden interest in reading the

paper?" my mother asked. "Is this an assignment for school or something?"

"No," I answered, trying to act cool about it. "I just figure I'm getting older now, and I should know more about what's happening in the world."

Boy! Were my parents ever impressed with *that* one! They practically shoved the paper at me.

"Good for you!" said my father. "This must mean you're finally growing up!"

Have you ever noticed that whenever you do something that your parents think is good, they suddenly decide you're "growing up"? Don't they *ever* think that you can do something good, and still be a kid?

After he handed me the paper, I went up to my room. Quickly, I turned to the classified ads. There must have been about a million ads in the paper that day! I had a *very* hard time finding the ad I had written. But finally, after about thirty minutes, I spotted the "personals" at the bottom of page six. And there it was.

WANTED: Nice young boy to live
with old couple. Call: 561-3447.

I checked it carefully to make sure it was exactly right. Perfect! Even the phone number was just the way I had written it. Naturally, I wasn't able to use the Hensons' *real* phone number in the ad. I didn't want any weirdos calling and asking them for a home. So when I wrote the ad I changed the last number. The Hensons' real phone number is 561-3446. But in the ad, I had put 561-3447. Brilliant, huh? I wondered what the poor people with the 3447 number would think when a bunch of stray boys started calling.

I stayed in my room a few more minutes, just staring at my ad. But finally I knew it was time to carry out Step Number Four. So I took a few deep breaths, braced myself, and headed back downstairs.

My parents were still in the kitchen, having their fiftieth cup of coffee.

"Mom! Take a look at what I found in the paper!" I said excitedly as I sat back down at the table. I opened the paper to the classifed ads.

"Look at what?" she asked, coming over to see what I was so interested in.

"Well, I was just looking through the ads to see if there was any cheap stuff for sale and I found this!" I explained.

I held out the ad for her to see. She read it out loud.

" 'Wanted: Nice young boy to live with old couple.' " Then she looked over at me and said, "So what?"

"So what?" I asked. "So don't you remember what I told you about the you-know-whos down the street?" I asked.

When my father heard me say "you-know-whos" he looked up.

"What in the world are you two talking about?" he asked, sounding a little bit hurt. Sometimes I think I should tell my father more secrets, just so he'll feel like he's part of the family.

My mother filled him in on all the things I had told her about the Hensons. Then together they took a closer took at my ad. They re-read it several times.

"Oh, those poor little old people," said my mother. "I just feel so sorry for them. Imagine, having to advertise for a boy to come and live with them. How sad."

"Wait a minute," said my father. "We don't even know for sure that the Hensons placed this ad. Maybe it was some other old couple."

I knew my father would say something like this. He always doubts everything. But I was ready.

"Why don't you just check the telephone number?" I suggested. "If it's the Hensons' number, that will prove it."

My mother got the phone book and looked up the Hensons' number. Then she checked it against the ad.

"Well?" asked my father.

"Oh dear," said my mother. "It's the Hensons' number all right. It looks like the paper made a mistake and printed a seven instead of a six. But all the other numbers are the same. I'm sure the Hensons must have placed that ad."

My parents talked about how sad this was for a few more minutes. I decided that if I didn't get out of there, I was going to burst with excitement!

"Well, I'll see you guys later," I said. "I think I'll go over to Tommy's and see if he's home from church."

Then I backed out the door and ran around into the front yard. I'm sure the smile on my face was so big you could have seen it a mile away! Step Number Four was over and all was well!

# Step Number Five

I waited until Tuesday night before I began work on my fifth step: "Put fake ad in paper from parents." The whole thing would be quite simple. All I needed to do was to make up another ad and call it into the paper by Wednesday afternoon.

I figured that Step Number Five wouldn't take much time, so after dinner I watched a couple of television shows. When they were over, I took a quick shower and then went straight to my room to prepare my next ad.

Just as I pulled out my secret notebook, I heard Robert pounding wildly on my door.

"Hey, Oscar, open up!" he shouted. "I've got something I want to show you!"

Quickly I shoved the notebook under some schoolbooks that were spread out on my desk. I didn't really want to let him in, but I figured he might get suspicious if I didn't.

"What do *you* want?" I asked as I unlocked the door. He was carrying a large shoe box.

"Look what Franklin Brady gave me!" he said excitedly. Carefully he lifted the lid to the box and let me peek in.

"Bugs—big deal," I said, seeing a bunch of little black things crawling around on the bottom. "What's so great about a box of bugs? You probably have more bugs than that living in your hair."

"That just shows how stupid you are, Oscar," he said. "For your dumb information, these are not just ordinary bugs. *Spiders* are not even members of the insect family. And these don't happen to be just plain old spiders, bug-brain. These are genuine black widows! Franklin got them from the science lab at school."

Then Robert opened the box again. But this time, instead of letting me peek inside, he turned the whole box upside down! Suddenly there were spiders everywhere!

"Oopsie! Sorry, Oscar!" he said with a stupid

smile on his face. "My, my, how clumsy of me."
Then he ran out of the room laughing, and shut
the door behind him.

"Robert! Robert!!!" I screamed. "You creep! You
get back here and get these things right now!"

I started for the door, but the spiders were
running all over. I decided the best thing I could
do was keep an eye on them. The thought of not
knowing where they were made me sick.

"Mom! Dad! Come quick! I need help!" I
screamed, as I watched one of them head for
my closet.

That's when it happened. "Yeow!" I shouted,
and looked down just in time to see another one
of the spiders running over my foot!

"Aaaauuuuugggggggg!" I screamed, again. "I've
been bitten! I've been bitten by a black widow!
Help!"

No one came. So I screamed and shouted
even louder.

"I'm dying! Somebody help me! Come quick!"

Still no one came. I continued to shout at the
top of my lungs for five solid minutes until finally my parents showed up at my door.

By the time they got there, I was on my bed, rolling around in pain. The foot that had been bitten was a little red and had started to puff up.

My parents walked into the room to see what was going on.

"So nice you guys could finally make it," I said, sounding *very* angry. "I'm sorry to tear you away from your TV program, but I seem to be having a slight problem here. Nothing to worry about, really. It's just that I'm dying."

"What in the world are you talking about?" my father said, sounding even angrier than I did. (He *hates* to called out of the room in the middle of a show.) "Quit acting like a jerk and tell us what all that ruckus was about?" he demanded.

"Well, excuse me for bothering you, Dad," I shouted. "I just figured that you and Mom would probably like to know that I won't be able to make it to breakfast tomorrow. I think that being dead takes your appetite away."

Both of them just stood there looking at me.

"Dead. Did you hear me?" I yelled. "Dead. That's spelled D-E-A-D, dead. As in, 'The boy is dead!' " Boy, was I ever mad.

My father started to look a little bit worried.

My mother sat down and took a look at my foot, which I was holding with both hands.

"What happened here?" she asked, pointing to the red mark.

"Oh, you mean that little thing there?" I said angrily. "That's nothing to worry about. It's just the mark black widows leave after they get finished killing you, that's all."

I've got to admit, even dying, I could be a pretty clever guy.

"A black widow?" asked my father. "That's ridiculous, Oscar. We don't even have black widows in this part of the country."

"That's what you think," I said. "Because for your information there happen to be several of them right in this room somewhere. And the fattest one just finished eating part of my foot."

Suddenly there was a great deal of giggling coming from out in the hall. And pretty soon Robert was standing in my doorway, doubled over laughing and clutching his sides.

"Do you know anything about this?" asked my father rather sternly.

That's when Robert fell on the floor. By this time he had laughed himself completely out of control. He rolled over and over, holding his sides.

"*Of course* he knows something about this!" I shouted. "*He's* the murderer who brought them in here! His jerky friend, Franklin Brady, stole them from the science lab at school!"

At this point I decided to stop shouting. I figured I didn't have much breath left, and I wanted to save as much strength as I could.

"By the way," I asked, "would anyone be interested in getting me to a hospital? Or would that make you miss too much of your television show?"

No one answered. They just kept watching as Robert rolled around and around on my floor in hysterics.

Finally I decided to do something to get their attention.

"Aauugg! Gasp!" I screeched. "Oh no! Mom . . . Dad . . . where are you? Everything is getting so dark in here! Did someone turn out the lights?"

When Robert heard this, he let out the biggest

scream of laughter you've ever heard in your life! He tried to say something, but he was having a hard time getting it out.

"They . . . hee, hee, ha, ha, ha hee . . . th-th-they weren't . . . giggle, giggle, haw, haw . . . black widows, you dummy!" he said finally. "They were j-just . . . hee, haw, haw . . . dumb little spiders from under the front porch!"

Well, it didn't take long before my parents figured out exactly what had happened. And neither one of them thought it was too funny, especially my father. He grabbed Robert by the feet and pulled him out of my room.

Robert was still laughing so hard, he didn't even care. As he was being pulled out the door he kept saying, "Did you hear him? He said, 'Everything is getting dark!'" Then Robert started laughing even harder than before.

I could have killed him! I wished it really had been a black widow bite. Believe me, dying would have been better than feeling as dumb as I was feeling.

My mother looked at my foot again and said, "Well, whatever it was, it bit you, all right. But I don't think you'll die. I'll go see what I can find to put on it."

While she was gone, my father came back into my room carrying a first-aid book. He pretended he was reading.

"Hmm," he said, "listen to this. To help heal spider bites, place a dead chicken over the wound."

"Dad!" I shouted. "It's not funny!"

"You're right," he said seriously. "I bet the chicken doesn't think so either."

"Dad!" I shouted again.

"Okay, okay," he said. "No need to yell. I was just trying to help."

Just then my mother walked back into my room carrying two cans. One was first-aid spray, and the other was insect spray.

I was afraid she was going to get mixed up and spray my foot with the wrong stuff, but she didn't. After she sprayed about a ton of first-aid spray on my spider bite, she took the other can and let the spiders have it.

"There!" she said after she had used up almost the whole can. "That ought to kill the rest of them."

The spiders didn't stand a chance. My room smelled so bad even I couldn't breathe. I started coughing.

"Kill *them?*" I asked disgustedly. "What about me?"

"This stuff doesn't hurt people, Oscar," she answered. "If you don't like the smell, just hold your breath."

"Great idea, Mother," I said. "Just great. If I don't breathe, I'll die for sure."

I wondered if my mother was going to let me get away with being a smart-aleck again, but when I looked up she didn't seem to be listening. She was just standing there like she was thinking about something. Then she hollered for Robert.

"Robert!" she shouted. "Get in here!"

Soon Robert showed up at the doorway. I figured that she was probably going to make him apologize. That's what he must have thought too.

Whenever we have a big fight, my mother always makes us say we're sorry. If you ask me, it's really dumb. When I clobber Robert the only thing I'm ever sorry about is that I didn't hit him harder.

Anyway, Robert stood there with his normal dumb face, holding his nose. He coughed once and said, "Sorry, Oscar." Then he started back to his room.

"Wait a minute, buddy," said my mother, grabbing hold of his shirt. (She was really mad. She never calls us "buddy" unless she's mad.) "I'm sure that you will want to do more to help Oscar than just say you're sorry. After all, because of you he's received a very painful spider bite. And now his room smells of bug spray. I really don't think that apologizing is going to do Oscar much good, do you?"

Robert looked just as confused as I felt.

"What am I supposed to do?" he asked.

"Go get your pajamas," ordered my mother. You could tell she meant business.

When Robert returned with his pajamas, he looked a little nervous.

"What are you going to do to me?" he asked my mother quietly.

"I'm going to let you and Oscar trade rooms tonight," she said cheerfully. "That way he'll be

able to breathe well enough to sleep. Rest is
*very* important when you've got an insect bite.
And I figure that Oscar will get a lot more sleep
if he doesn't have to breathe in all these fumes."

"What about me?" asked Robert.

"*You*, my dear boy, are not the one with the
bite, are you?"

From the way she said it, I could tell my
mother was *really* enjoying herself.

I gathered up my homework books. Then I
pranced out of the room, trying to look as jolly
as I possibly could.

"Nighty-night, Robert," I said, as I bounded
out of the room.

"He doesn't look too sick to me," Robert said
to my mother. At least that's what I *think* he
said. I really couldn't tell because he was holding his nose and the words sounded funny.

I loved it! Finally, after all these years, my
good old mother had come through for me!

By this time it was getting pretty late, but I
still had to write that ad for the newspaper.
After I went into Robert's room, I locked the
door and took out my notebook.

I started writing. This ad was a lot easier to

write than the first one. I didn't take long at all to decide what I wanted to say. It was simple . . .

WANTED: Good clean home for helpful young boy. Call: 568-6990.

"Perfect!" I said, smiling to myself. "This is just perfect!"

Then I crawled under the covers. My foot was still throbbing a little, but still I was able to smile. Down the hall, I heard Robert cough.

I laughed out loud.

# Step Number Six

The next morning I put some extra money in my pocket. On the way to school I stopped by the gas station and used their pay phone to call the newspaper and place my ad. I made the same arrangements to pay.

After that, it was just a matter of waiting for the week to end so I could finish off the sixth step: "Show fake ad to Hensons."

This time the week went by pretty fast. Before I knew it, another Sunday had rolled around. And, for the third straight week in a row, I asked my parents if I could take the Sunday paper up to my room after breakfast. By now they had probably begun to think that I was just about the brightest kid in the whole school.

I had no trouble finding my ad this time. It was on the third page.

As I read it, I tingled with excitement! I got the scissors and cut the ad out of the paper so I could show it to the Hensons. Then I went back downstairs and gave the paper back to my mother.

"Thanks, honey," she said. "I wanted to take a look at the classified ads. I was wondering if there might be another ad in there from the Hensons."

Geez! Was I in trouble now! If she looked at the ads and saw a big space cut out of the page, she'd *really* be suspicious!

"Oh no! Don't do that!" I said, panicking.

"Why not, Oscar? What's wrong with you?" she asked.

"Me? Why nothing," I said with a laugh. "It's just that . . . well . . . ah . . . I already looked to see if it was in there, and it's not. Honest! So you might as well just save yourself the trouble."

Unfortunately, my mother is one of those people who always has to see everything for herself. She started to pick it up.

"Wait!" I screamed. "Don't touch that paper! Put it down!"

I shouted so loud, she dropped the paper on the floor.

Quickly, I gathered it up into a big crumpled ball and began swatting the floor with it.

At first my mother just stood there looking at me. I think she was afraid that this time I had really cracked.

Finally she pulled herself together.

"What the hell are you doing, Oscar?" she asked angrily.

This was only the eighth time in my whole life that my mother had ever said the word "hell." I know. I keep a record of all the bad words she says. That way, if she ever hears *me* cussing, I can pull out my record and show her all the times that she has cussed too.

I also started to keep a cussing record on my father. But by the end of the first month I had already run out of pages, so I decided to give up on him.

Anyway, I finally stopped swatting the floor with the paper and looked up.

"Didn't you see it?" I asked.

"See what? What are you talking about?" asked my mother, still *very* annoyed.

"Geez, Mother!" I said. "You mean to tell me that you didn't see that disgusting bug crawling up the paper? It looked like one of those centipedes. Aren't those the things with all those hairy legs?"

Was I brilliant, or was I brilliant?

"Oh, Oscar, you're kidding! I'm sorry, honey," she said. "I didn't even see it. I just couldn't figure out what you were doing."

"That's okay," I answered. "By the way, I'm sorry about the paper, Mom."

We both looked down at the floor. The paper was laying there in a big crumpled pile. It was torn to shreds. I had really done an excellent job!

"Oh well," said my mother, "I guess it doesn't really matter anyway. You said the Hensons' ad wasn't in there, didn't you?"

"Yes," I answered. "And, believe me, Mother, I looked everywhere for it!" Moving toward the door, I added, "Well, if it's okay with you, I think I'll go outside for a while and see if I can find somebody to play with."

"Why don't you and Robert go down to the schoolyard and play some ball?" asked my mother.

"No offense, Mom," I said. "But in case you haven't noticed, I don't care much for Robert."

She just sighed. Whenever my mother doesn't know what to say, she sighs.

As I shut the door, I heard her shout something at me. But this time I kept on going. I had a feeling she wanted to give me another lecture on how "We're a Family and We're All Supposed to Love Each Other." And, frankly, I just wasn't in the mood for it.

As I walked toward the Hensons' house, I didn't see anyone around. That really bothered me. I didn't want to have to knock on the door. If there's one thing I can't stand doing, it's knocking on doors.

Whenever I knock on someone's door, I never know quite what to do while I'm waiting for them to come. Usually I just stand there staring at the doorknob. It really makes me feel like an idiot. But if no one's home, I feel even worse. I just sort of slump over and wander away.

All the while I was walking to the Hensons', I kept hoping that by the time I got there Mr. Henson would be out puttering in his yard. But no such luck. No one was in sight. So I just stood there for a while, hanging around their steps.

Finally I got up my nerve. I forced myself to

march up their front steps and knock on the door. I figured I'd knock once. Then when Mr. Henson came to the door, I would act real sad and ask if I could speak to him for a minute.

Once I had made my decision, I pounded heavily on the screen door. I waited nervously. But no one came.

I pounded louder. This time I heard someone coming down the stairs.

"Why, hello there, Oscar," said Mrs. Henson as she opened the screen door. "What brings you here?"

Geez! I hadn't expected *Mrs.* Henson. It really took me by surprise.

"Ah . . . well . . . ah . . . Mrs. Henson," I stuttered, "I was just wondering . . . ah . . . do you think Mr. Henson can come out and play?"

Geez! What a dumb thing to say! I felt my face turning red.

Mrs. Henson just giggled. "Wait a minute, Oscar," she said. "I'll tell him you're here."

"Thanks a lot," I said. "I'll just sit here on the front porch."

If I had one wish in the whole world, I think I

would wish that nothing dumb would ever come out of my mouth again.

As I sat there and waited, I prayed that Mrs. Henson would not tell her husband that I had asked if he could play. I really prayed!

Suddenly the door opened.

"Does someone out here want me to come out and play?" said Mr. Henson, chuckling.

Thanks a lot, God, I said to myself.

"Oh, hi, Mr. Henson," I said out loud. "It's only me. I just thought I'd come over and talk to you for a minute. I hope I'm not bothering you or anything."

"Not at all," he answered. "What's on your mind, young fella?"

"Well, Mr. Henson," I began, "I just wanted to thank you for keeping the secret I told you. I really appreciate having someone to talk to about it."

Mr. Henson looked a bit upset.

"I've been very worried about your family," he said, putting his arm around me. "I wish there was something Mrs. Henson and I could do to help out. It makes me sad to think your family is going through such a bad time right now." Then he patted me on the head.

"Have you read today's paper yet?" I asked.

"That's just what I was doing when you knocked," he answered.

"Oh, then I guess you haven't seen *this*, have you?" I asked, taking the little ad out of my pocket. "Take a look at this, Mr. Henson," I said sadly. "I found it in today's classified ads."

Mr. Henson started to read my ad out loud. "Wanted: Good clean home for helpful young boy."

Suddenly, Mr. Henson's face looked very strange—almost as if he might cry.

"Oh my goodness," he said, softly, shaking his head. "You don't mean . . . you're not trying to tell me . . . do you mean to say that your parents placed this ad, young fella?"

Slowly, I nodded my head. Then I sniffed.

"They're trying to find a good home for Robert," I said sadly.

"Are you positive that your parents placed it, and not someone else?" he asked. "I mean, is this your phone number here on this ad?"

Once again, I had been *very* careful about the phone number.

"Well," I began, "it's *almost* my number. The paper must have made a mistake and printed 568-6990 instead of 568-6999. But, it's close enough, Mr. Henson. I'm *sure* that ad is from my parents. They're trying to find someone who will take Robert in for free."

I watched his face as he read the ad over and over again. I could tell he believed me. In a way, I felt kind of bad. I really hated lying to a person as nice as Mr. Henson. But it simply had to be done. If I didn't get rid of Robert soon, I knew I would lose my mind.

After a few minutes of sitting there in silence, Mr. Henson got up.

"Well, young fella, I've got a few things to do inside. And I hope you don't mind, but I think it's time for me to tell Mrs. Henson about the problems your poor family is having. Mrs. Henson is very good at solving problems, you know."

I got up to leave. "Sure, that would be okay, Mr. Henson," I said. "Just be sure to tell her not to mention any of this to my parents, or to

Robert. Poor little Robert. He breaks into tears every time it's mentioned."

Mr. Henson smiled a sad smile.

"We'll figure something out, young fella," he said. "Don't you worry. Everything's going to be okay."

Then he turned and went inside.

As I walked back home, I was smiling like a real idiot. The sixth step had gone as smoothly as all the others.

I breathed a huge sigh of relief. Only two steps to go before my life would be Robert-less!

# Steps Number Seven and Eight

I waited about a week before starting the next step of my operation. I wanted to give the Hensons plenty of time to think about the terrible problems I had told them our family was having.

During this time I also had to make sure that my family didn't forget about the "poor Hensons." Every day I mentioned their name and talked about how tired old Mrs. Henson must be getting. As a matter of fact, I talked about them so much that I got sick of them.

By the time the week had ended, I was more than ready to get on with the seventh step: "Write fake letter to Hensons."

It was Saturday morning and I had baseball practice. But as soon as it was over, I rushed home.

"Mom!" I hollered as I ran in the door. "I need to borrow your typewriter. I have to do a report for school."

"Okay, Oscar," she answered. "But be sure you don't break it. It's not a toy. You'll have to be very careful!"

I hate it when she says stuff like that! How would she like it if I said, "Mom, please don't touch anything in my room. I'm really afraid you'll break something. You know what a big oaf you are."

"I won't break it," I shouted disgustedly. "Don't worry, Mom. Clumsy old Oscar will be careful."

I carried the typewriter up to my room and began working. I had planned to type the letters for Step Number Seven and Step Number Eight before lunch. Unfortunately, I hadn't realized how long typing such a short letter could take. I guess using only one finger really slows you down. By twelve-thirty I was just finishing up my first letter. It went like this:

Dear Mr. and Mrs. Henson,

Our wonderful son, Oscar, told us that you know how poor our family has become. Please don't worry about us. We'll be just fine as soon as we get rid of someone. We just can't afford to feed four people right now.

If you know of anyone who would like to have our darling little son come live with them, please let us know.

Thank goodness Oscar eats like a bird.

> Sincerely,
> Mr. and Mrs. Winkle

After I was finished, I read the letter over again. I was very pleased with myself. It was just perfect. I had even used my mother's best typing paper. If anything would get the Hensons to take Robert, this letter would. I was sure.

I was so excited about how well everything was going that I decided to skip lunch and get started on the eighth step: "Write fake letter to parents."

The second letter didn't take nearly as long to write. I guess I was just getting very good at this sort of thing. Before long, the letter to my parents was all ready to go. It said:

Dear Mr. and Mrs. Winkle,

I guess your wonderful son, Oscar, told you about all our problems. Please don't worry about us. I'm sure we'll be all right as soon as we find a nice boy to come stay with us. I just hope my poor, old, tired, back holds up that long.

Lucky for you you've got those two strong sons. That little Robert's such a joy.

Sincerely,

Mrs. Henson

P.S. Mr. Henson was going to write this letter, but he fell asleep in the vegetable garden again.

Perfect! Perfect! Perfect! This letter was even better than the first one!

After I finished typing, I folded both letters neatly and stuffed them into envelopes. I was *very* careful not to get the letters mixed up. I typed "Mr. and Mrs. Henson" on the outside of the first letter, and "Mr. and Mrs. Winkle" on the outside of the second. Then I hid both letters under my mattress. I would "deliver" them on Monday.

I took the typewriter back downstairs to my mother.

"You didn't break anything, did you, honey?" she asked.

"Why do you always have to ask me that?" I asked. "Why is it that you think I will break everything I touch? I'm not a clumsy little kid anymore, you know!"

Just then, Robert came in the front door.

"Speaking of clumsy little kids," I said, "here comes one now!"

"Shut up, Oscar the Grouch," said Robert.

Honestly, the kid just doesn't have any sense of humor at all.

"Make me, Robert the Slobert," I answered.

I'm not really sure why I started picking on him. Sometimes, I think I just do it out of habit. It's sort of like biting your nails. You get started and it's hard to stop.

"How did practice go, Robert?" asked my mother. Whenever my mother thinks there's going to be a fight, she tries to change the subject.

"Okay," answered Robert. "But my coach said I need a little more practice hitting. I was wondering if maybe you or Dad could pitch me a few balls?"

"I'm pretty busy now, Robert," said my mom. "And Dad won't be back for three or four hours. Why don't you ask your brother. Maybe if you ask him real nicely, he might pitch some balls to you out in the back yard."

Geez! I hate that! My mother does this kind of thing all the time. I'm standing right there, and she pretends that she and Robert are all alone, talking about me! She acts like I'm deaf! It's insulting!

All she has to do is say, "Oscar, would you mind pitching Robert some balls?" That's all she has to do.

Then Robert turned to me and said, "Oscar . . . would . . . "

"I *know*, Robert," I said, interrupting. "I *heard* the question already. The reason I *heard* the question already is that I'm standing right here. This may come as a big shock to our mother, but my hearing is *fine*."

My mother ignored me.

Anyway, I figured Robert must *really* need help if he would consider asking *me*. So I decided to be a wonderful brother and help him. I've got to admit, when Robert's really trying to be nice, I don't mind helping him out once in a while. The problem is, he's only been nice fourteen times in his whole life. I *know*. I keep a record of *that*, too.

The two of us went outside and I threw Robert a few balls. Right away I knew why his coach was upset. The kid stunk.

No matter where I threw the ball, Robert kept swinging the bat like a golf club. Even when I threw it way over his head, he swung the bat on the ground.

He looked so ridiculous, I could hardly keep from laughing. But I knew if I laughed, he wouldn't want to practice. And I simply could not have any brother of mine going to a game and swinging like an idiot. The first thing you know, people would start thinking he had learned it from me.

I stayed out back helping Robert the whole afternoon. I showed him a better way to hold the bat. And I made him keep his eye on the ball. After about three hours of work, he finally started getting some real good hits.

My mother was so excited to see us playing together that she brought out this big pitcher of grape Kool-Aid. I think she got the idea from watching a television commercial. She even tried to draw that smiling face on the pitcher. It didn't work, though. It just looked all smeary.

Anyway, she poured us each a big glass of Kool-Aid and gave us cookies. As we ate them, she stood there smiling. It really made me feel like a fool.

After I finished our little "treat" (as my mother kept calling it), I went back inside. Robert didn't come right away. He was still too busy slugging down more Kool-Aid.

Finally, when he came in, he had this big purple stain all over his mouth from the Kool-Aid. He really looked ridiculous.

"Yuck!" I said, pointing to his mouth. "There's a fungus among us!" I started laughing.

Robert didn't seem to think this was quite as funny as I did. What did I tell you? *No* sense of humor.

"Shut up, you Oscar Mayer Wiener!" he shouted. He knows how much I hate that.

"What's the matter Slobert?" I said. "Can't you take a joke?"

To tell you the truth, I was glad Robert and I were back to acting normal. I get nervous when Robert stays nice for too long. It makes me think he's flipped out or something. Besides, I don't think I could drink much more Kool-Aid, with my mother standing around grinning. It's really corny.

# Delivery Day

After another boring Sunday had gone by, I was really glad when Monday finally came.

"Today is Delivery Day!" I said out loud as I got up. I knew that I was almost at the end of Operation: Dump the Chump! It wouldn't be long now before Robert was out of my hair for good.

It was the last week of school, so there wasn't much work left to be done. Most of the time we played games. We had to write a composition called "My Summer Plans." I could hardly write mine. All I could think about was having the entire summer with no Robert!

After school I ran right home and got the envelope that was addressed to the Hensons. I put it in my back pocket and told my mother I was going out to play.

As I headed down the street, I could see Mr. and Mrs. Henson sitting outside on their front porch.

"Hi, Mr. and Mrs. Henson," I called as I neared the house.

"Hello, Oscar," said Mrs. Henson smiling.

"Hi there, young fella," said Mr. Henson.

I walked up the steps to their porch. Then, as I took the envelope out of my back pocket, I gave them each a sad little smile.

"Here, Mr. Henson," I said. "My mother said to give this to you."

Mr. Henson looked rather puzzled as he took the envelope. He started reading, and I sat down on the step to wait for him to finish.

"Do you know what this letter says, young fella?" he asked when he was done.

"Yes, Mr. Henson," I answered sadly. "My mother read it to me before I brought it over."

Mrs. Henson was trying to see what was in the letter. "Read it out loud to me, George," she said to Mr. Henson. "I left my glasses in the house."

Slowly Mr. Henson picked up the letter.

"Dear Mr. and Mrs. Henson." he read out loud.

"Our wonderful son, Oscar, told us that you know how poor our family has become. Please don't worry about us. We'll be just fine as soon as we get rid of someone. We just can't afford to feed four people right now.

"If you know of anyone who would like to have our darling little son come live with them, please let us know.

"Thank goodness Oscar eats like a bird."

Mr. Henson looked up at his wife and said, "And it's signed 'Mr. and Mrs. Winkle.' "

"Oh my!" said Mrs. Henson loudly. "Oh my!"

For the next few minutes, all of us just sat there on the porch looking real sad. Then Mrs. Henson asked her husband to read the note over one more time.

When he was finished, Mrs. Henson looked a little bit confused. I could tell that something about the note bothered her.

"What's wrong, Mrs. Henson?" I asked. If she had any questions, I decided I might as well answer them now.

"Nothing's really wrong, Oscar," she said. "It's

just that your mother used the term 'get rid of.' Trying to find a home for a child isn't really the same thing as trying to get rid of him. It just seems strange that she would put it that way."

I felt myself panicking again, "Ah . . . well, that's probably because you haven't been around my mother that much, Mrs. Henson," I blurted. "My mother says 'get rid of' all the time. And besides, you should have seen how upset she was when she wrote this note. I bet she didn't even know what she was writing!"

"Of course," said Mrs. Henson. "She was probably just upset."

Whew! That was a close one! I decided I'd better get out of there before I blew the whole thing. But first something else needed to be said.

"Boy, Mr. and Mrs. Henson," I began. "Wouldn't it be great if you knew someone who was real old and needed a kid around to help out? Wouldn't that be perfect? I bet my mother wouldn't feel half as bad about getting rid of her kid if she thought she was helping out some old people. You two don't happen to know any old people, do you?" I asked.

Mr. Henson smiled. "We might know a couple," he said.

"Well, if you think of anyone, please let me know," I said.

I stood up and started to leave. "There's just one more thing," I added.

"What is it, young fella?" asked Mr. Henson.

"Well," I said, "just in case you might feel like talking to my mother about this note, you'd better not call her till later. She's probably still busy crying right now."

"You sure are considerate of your mother's feelings, Oscar," said Mrs. Henson. "I think it's just wonderful the way you keep trying to protect her."

"Thanks," I said. "But my mother's not the only one. I've got to protect my dad's feelings too. That's why I've asked you to keep all this a secret. If you ever said anything to him about getting fired, he'd really be upset.

The Hensons stood up to go inside.

"Don't worry, young fella," said Mr. Henson. "Mrs. Henson and I would never say anything to embarrass your father."

"Thanks," I said. "I knew I could count on you." And as I turned to leave, I added, "Well, I guess I'd better go now. I want to find out if Robert's found himself a place to live yet. Nice places are hard to find. And good old Robert is such a great little kid, we have to make sure he gets a real nice family."

"So long, Mr. and Mrs. Henson," I finished with a wave. "And thanks for being so nice."

I hurried home. There was only one more thing that needed to be done. After that, it would be up to the Hensons.

When I got to my house, I rushed upstairs and grabbed the other letter. Quickly, I put it in my pocket and ran down to the kitchen to give it to my mother.

By the time I got there, I was almost out of breath. But I had to hurry in case the Hensons called.

"Here, Mom," I said, handing her the envelope. "This is for you. I just came from the Hensons'. Mrs. Henson asked me to give this to you."

My mother sat down at the kitchen table and opened the letter. She began reading.

When she was all finished, she looked up.

"Oh dear, those poor, poor, sweet old people," she said. "What are we going to do about them?"

"Read it to me, Mom," I said. "You know how much I care about those poor, poor, sweet old people."

She read the letter again, out loud:

"Dear Mrs. and Mr. Winkle," she began.

"I guess your wonderful son, Oscar, told you about all our problems. Please don't worry about us. I'm sure we'll be all right as soon as we find a nice boy to come stay with us. I just hope my poor, old, tired back holds up that long.

"Lucky for you you've got those two strong sons. That little Robert's such a joy.

"Sincerely, Mrs. Henson.

"P.S. Mr. Henson was going to write this letter, but he fell asleep in the vegetable garden again."

My mother put down the letter and turned to me. "Oh Oscar," she said sadly. "I just feel so bad for those poor folks. As soon as your father gets home, I'm going to show him this letter. There's just got to be something we can do to help them."

My father got home soon after that. I hung around the kitchen door and listened while my mother showed him the letter.

I felt very relieved to have everything over with. I wasn't sure exactly what would happen next, but whatever it was, I hoped it would happen soon. I just couldn't stand to wait much longer.

That night, at dinner, things started off great. As soon as I sat down, my parents began talking about the Hensons and all their problems. Boy, was I excited! I knew exactly what they were trying to lead up to. My mother even talked about how good it makes you feel when you help others.

Unfortunately, Robert didn't seem to be listening at all. He just kept stuffing his face and sloshing down milk.

"What do you boys think we could do to help the Hensons?" asked my father.

Robert finally looked up from his plate. I guess he decided to come up for air.

"The Hensons?" he asked. "What's wrong with the Hensons?"

Geez! What a jerk! For weeks I had been talking about how poor and weak Mr. Henson was, and my jerky brother still couldn't figure out why they needed help!

"The Hensons are getting old, you jerk!" I said. "And they need someone to help out. But they don't have enough money to hire anyone. Geez, Robert, don't you listen to anything that goes on around here? You probably don't even know how much the Hensons like you. They think you're just about the neatest kid in the whole world," I added.

Robert looked surprised. "The Hensons like me?" he said. "I didn't know they liked me."

"Like you?" I said. "Robert, those poor old people practically love you!"

He seem puzzled. "Why in the world would they love me?" he asked. "I hardly even know them any more. That makes me feel kind of spooky . . . having people love me that I hardly even know."

I couldn't believe that Robert was saying

those terrible things about the Hensons right in front of my parents!

I knew if I let him keep talking, it wouldn't be long before my parents would give up on the idea of sending him down there. I had to find a way to shut him up!

"Robert!" I said, "why don't you just—"

Suddenly, before I had a chance to finish, the telephone rang.

My heart began to pound wildly! I hoped this was the call I had been waiting for!

My father got up and answered it. I listened closely to his side of conversation.

"Why hello, Mr. Henson!" he said. "How nice to hear from you! We were just talking about you folks. How are you feeling?"

My stomach was doing flip-flops. I prayed that my father wouldn't ask about Mrs. Henson's back.

"What's that, Mr. Henson?" he asked. "Well, thank you. Yes, we think he's a pretty special little boy, too. I understand he feels the same way about you."

This must have been the part where Mr. Henson was telling my father how much they liked Robert! I knew good old Mr. Henson wouldn't let me down!

I waited as Mr. Henson did some more talking. I wished desperately that I could hear what he was saying on the other end of the phone. Then my father spoke again.

"Mr. Henson, we'll have to finish talking it over before we can give you a definite answer. But I just have a feeling that he's not going to mind a bit. As a matter of fact, Mr. Henson, I think he'll be delighted. Yes, well, thank you very much, Mr. Henson. Why don't you call back in about an hour? Okay then. Bye."

After he hung up, my father came back to the table and sat down. He looked at my mother and nodded his head.

My mother smiled as though she already knew what was happening. They must have already talked it over. I'll bet they weren't even surprised to get Mr. Henson's phone call.

I looked at Robert. He was still cramming his face full of food. I would have loved to see the look on his face when my parents told him he'd be moving in with the Hensons for the summer. But I didn't dare stick around. I knew I wouldn't be able to keep from cracking up when they told him the news. And now was no time for anyone to become suspicious!

"Excuse me, please," I said to my mother. "I've got a few things to do in my room. I think I'll just leave you three to talk alone."

As I got up, I gave my mother a wink. I wanted her to know I was grown up enough to know what was going on.

I ran up to my room as fast as I could. I almost didn't get there soon enough! Screams of joy began to come out of my mouth just as I hit the door!

"Whoopee!" I shouted, flinging myself down on my bed. "Yeeee-haaaa!" I screamed into my pillow.

"Bye-bye, Slobert Robert!" I said right out loud.

Operation: Dump the Chump was completed! And everything had gone perfectly!

# Good-bye Robert!

After about thirty minutes, I went back downstairs to see what had happened. When I walked into the kitchen, Robert was nowhere to be found.

My parents were cleaning up the dishes. My mother turned and smiled when I came into the room. My father did the same thing.

"Where did Robert go?" I asked, as if I didn't know.

I was sure he was up in his room packing his suitcases. He was also probably crying. The thought made me giggle.

"He went out for a little while, Oscar," said my mother.

Then she came over and sat down beside me.

"Honey, there's something very important that your father and I would like to discuss with you. It's about the Hensons, Oscar."

"I already know what you're going to tell me, Mom," I said interrupting. "And I know it's probably hard to have one of your kids move out. But really, Mom, the Hensons are great people. In fact, they're just about the nicest people I know. Except for you and Dad of course."

"Oh, Oscar," said my mother, leaning over to give me a kiss. "Your father and I are so proud of the way you're taking this. I was really afraid that you might be lonely without Robert."

"Have you told Robert?" I asked excitedly.

"Yes," she answered. "He heard us talking about it after dinner."

"What did he say?" I asked, trying to control the smile on my face.

"He was so cute," said my mother. "He said he was going to miss you."

Now, I've got to admit, that made me feel kind of bad. Here, I had spent all that time trying to dump Robert, and the first thing he says is how much he'll miss me when he's gone.

"Dad, exactly what did Mr. Henson say when he called?" I asked. My curiosity was killing me.

"Well, first he started off by saying how much he's liked you boys all these years. Then, he said that sometimes he and Mrs. Henson wish they had someone to help fill up that big old house of theirs. He even said how much they love to hear the sound of children's laughter."

Good old Mr. Henson, I thought to myself. Good old *dependable* Mr. Henson!

"What else did he say, Dad?" I asked again.

"Hmmm," he said. "Let's see. Oh, then, he said how he and Mrs. Henson would love it if we would ever consider letting one of you boys come stay with them for a while. He really seems like a wonderful man, Oscar," he said.

"Yeah, he *really* is," I agreed.

"And, the best thing about it," said my mother, "is that Mr. Henson wasn't ashamed to ask us for help. Even though he doesn't know us that well, he seemed to know that we were the kind of people he could count on! That really makes me feel good. Do you know what I mean, Oscar?"

"Yes, I do, Mom," I answered. "I really do."

Then my mother reached over and hugged me. And as she sat there squeezing me, she said something that made me feel sick to my stomach.

"We're really going to miss you around here this summer, Oscar," she said quietly.

# The End?

Don't ask me how everything got so messed up last night. It was as big a surprise to me as it was to anyone.

Where did I go wrong? Where did I go wrong? I must have asked myself that question a thousand times.

Where in the world did Mr. and Mrs. Henson ever get the idea that I should be the one to come live with them? Didn't they listen to all that good stuff I said about Robert? What's wrong with them anyway? Can't they hear? Maybe that's what happens when you get a lot of hair growing in your ears.

But that's no excuse for my parents. I've checked. And neither one of them has any hair in their ears at all. I know they heard me tell them over and over again how much the Hensons loved Robert. Not me—Robert! Not once did I ever mention that the Hensons even *liked* me!

And why, all of a sudden, do my parents decide they have to help our neighbors? They've never helped anyone out before. What a fine time for them to decide to be nice.

Last night after my mother told me the "news," I ran straight up to my room to try to figure a way out of the mess I was in. I immediately ruled out telling the truth. I would rather spend the rest of my life at the Hensons' than let Robert know how my plan had gone wrong. If Robert knew the truth, he would never be able to stop laughing. He'd probably even have to drop out of school because he'd be laughing too hard to go. No—now was definitely not the time for honesty.

I decided to try psychology. I found Robert and called him into my room.

"Gee, Robert, too bad," I said. "You lose again. Looks like you'll have to spend another boring summer hanging around the house. Maybe when you grow up a little you'll be able to go away for the summer just like me." This was supposed to get Robert to beg to change places with me.

"Yeah," said Robert, "spending the summer with a couple of old people sounds like a lot of fun all right. Maybe next year Mom and Dad will let you spend the summer at a nursing home. I bet you'd really have a ball there." Then he walked out of my room laughing.

So much for psychology.

Finally, I didn't know what else to do, so I started crying. I hid my head in my pillow so no one could hear me.

After a couple of minutes I heard the phone ring. I knew it was Mr. Henson calling back to find out if I was going to be able to come.

My mother picked up the phone in the kitchen. I opened my door and tried to listen, but I couldn't hear what she was saying. It's too bad, too. Because while they were talking, something went very, very wrong.

After about ten minutes had passed, my mother came up to my room. But she didn't come in. Instead, she just stood in my doorway with her arms crossed and this real mean look on her face.

"Mr. Henson is on the phone," she said, sounding very angry. "He wants to speak to you."

I just couldn't figure it out. What had happened to make her so mad?

I went into my parents' bedroom and picked up the phone. My mother was right behind me. She was still wearing her mean look and her arms were still folded. She was making me very uncomfortable.

"Hello?" I said into the receiver.

"Well, hi there, young fella!" said Mr. Henson. "Your mother just told me the good news!"

Poor Mr. Henson. I felt kind of sorry for him. He really thought he was doing us a big favor.

"Are you getting all packed for the summer?" he asked. "Your mother said you'd be coming as soon as school gets out."

I took a deep breath. It was really hard trying to act happy.

"Well," I answered, "I haven't started to pack yet. I'll probably do a little tomorrow."

"Great," he said. "We just can't wait. By the

way, how's your mother taking this? I hope I didn't embarrass her by what I said."

Oh no! I thought. So *that's* it. Mr. Henson said something to spill the beans! I had to find out what it was.

"Ah . . . what do you mean, 'embarrass' her?" I asked nervously.

I looked over at my mother. She didn't look embarrassed at all. Mad. She looked very, very mad.

"Well," said Mr. Henson, "I know that you asked me not to mention anything to your father about how he lost his job, but I didn't think it would matter if I discussed it with your mother. I hope I didn't upset her."

I felt my heart stop beating.

"Ah . . . exactly wh-what d-did you say, Mr. Henson?" I stuttered.

"Oh, nothing much," he answered. "I was just trying to make her feel better. So I told her that Mrs. Henson and I thought it was just awful the way his boss fired him. And I also told her that I would do anything I could to help him find another job."

"A-another j-job?" I repeated.

Once again I looked at my mother. She waved. It was a mean wave.

"Ah . . . gee, Mr. Henson, that's really nice of you," I mumbled under my breath.

Mr. Henson continued talking. "Listen, young fella," he said, "before we hang up, I wanted to check and see if you'll be able to come on our vacation with us. We have a place at the beach that's been in the family for years. It's not very fancy, but we always have a good time there. We usually go for most of the summer. If you'd like to go, I'll talk to your parents about it. Do you think they would mind if we took you away for that long?"

I glanced at my mother for the third time. She looked like she wouldn't mind if the Hensons took me away for the rest of my life.

"No, Mr. Henson," I said. "I have a feeling that they wouldn't mind a bit."

"That's just great!" he exclaimed. "I'll talk to them about it later. Well, I guess that's about it. I'll hang up now and we'll see you in a few days. Mrs. Henson is going to bake one of her delicious cherry pies to celebrate!"

I hung up. My mother followed me back to my room. She just kept staring. I wasn't sure whether she had figured out my whole plan. But one thing was certain. She knew a lot more than I ever wanted her to know.

"Ah . . . boy . . . you know, that old Mr. Henson really gets some funny ideas in his head," I said trying to explain. "Like . . . well, do you know what he just told me? He told me that he was going to help Dad find another job. Isn't that funny?"

"Ha ha," said my mother. Only it was a real disgusted "ha ha."

"I mean, isn't it funny how old people get confused about stuff?" I asked again.

"Funny," said my mother.

"Well, I guess it's a good thing I'll be staying with them for a while, isn't it? That way I'll be able to help them if they get confused about anything else."

"How very kind," said my mother.

"Yeah, well, I guess I'd better be getting some sleep now," I said. I walked over to the doorway where my mother was standing and turned out my light. I kissed her good night and got into bed.

My mother just stood there in the dark.

"Ah . . . is something wrong?" I asked finally.

"Wrong?" she asked. "Wrong? Heavens no, Oscar. What could possibly be wrong?"

No doubt about it. She was really mad.

"Well, okay then," I said. "If nothing's wrong, I'll just close my eyes and try to get some sleep. Good night."

She didn't leave.

"Oscar," she said finally, "if you don't mind, there is one teeny, tiny, little question that I would like to ask you before I go."

"Ah . . . okay," I said nervously. "What's the question?"

"HOW STUPID DO I LOOK, OSCAR?" she yelled. "JUST HOW STUPID DO I LOOK?"

Boy! She was even madder than I thought.

"Answer me!" she shouted again.

"Ah . . . how stupid do you look?" I babbled nervously. "Well . . . I don't know . . . I mean it's so dark in here I really can't see you very well."

"Well, I certainly hope that your eyes get better this summer," she said angrily. "Because when you come home again, I want you to take a very good look at me. And if I still look stupid, we'll have them tested. Because believe it or not, Oscar, I'm not quite the idiot you think I am. Do you understand what I'm saying?"

"Yes," I answered quietly.

"I don't know exactly what you've done, Oscar," she continued. "And to tell you the truth, I don't even think I want to. I have a feeling that if I knew the whole story, I would be even more mad than I am right now. And if I was any madder, I would probably explode."

"Maybe we should talk about this tomorrow after you've had a chance to calm down," I suggested.

"Tomorrow?" she said loudly. "Tomorrow? Oh no, Oscar. Tomorrow we won't have a chance to talk. As soon as you come home from school we're going to have to start packing. It takes a long time to pack when you're going to be away for the whole summer. And believe me, Oscar, you really *are* going. For some reason the Hensons seem very excited about it. And I wouldn't disappoint those sweet people now for the world."

"I know," I said. "They wanted to know if I could go to the beach with them this summer."

"As far as I'm concerned, you could go to the moon with them Oscar," said my mother. Then she turned quickly and stomped out of the room. She didn't even kiss me good night. In a way, I was glad. I have a feeling it would have been a very mean kiss.

After she left, I lay there thinking about how botched up everything was. If only Mr. Henson hadn't tried to be so nice. Why did he have to go and say he would help my father get a job? Oh well, there wasn't much I could do about it then, so I just went to sleep.

As soon as I got home from school this afternoon my mother did exactly what she'd said she would do. She brought the suitcases to my room, flopped them on my bed, and started packing.

I guess I might as well get used to the idea. I'm spending the summer at the beach. And that's that.

Robert's going to day camp. I was going to go too, but I guess that's off now. I don't really mind. I hated day camp last year. Robert spent most of his time humiliating me. I remember one time when we were canoeing, he stood up and pretended he was George Washington crossing the Delaware. The boating instructor saw him and made us beach our canoe for the rest of the week.

I wonder if the Hensons have a boat. If they don't, maybe they would take me on one of those deep-sea cruises for a day. That would really be neat. Actually, I guess the beach can be a lot of fun. Usually there are lots of lonely kids running around looking for someone to play with.

I better ask my mother if I can take our good canvas raft. She doesn't seem quite as mad this afternoon. She keeps bringing in all this stuff she wants me to pack. Most of it's stuff for good grooming. A minute ago she even brought in this dumb little manicure set for my fingernails.

Hmm . . . look at this thing. Look at those tiny little scissors. Maybe I'll show them to Mr. Henson. I'll bet they're just what he's been needing for those ear hairs.

I wonder what Mr. Henson does with his teeth when he swims? He probably doesn't wear them because the waves would knock them out of his mouth. Geez, I hope he doesn't leave them on the blanket!

That reminds me. I'd better find my bathing suit. And my kite—I'll need that. There's usually a pretty good wind on the beach at night.

Well, maybe this summer will be better than I thought. After all, I guess a whole entire summer without Robert can't be all bad.

Too bad he'll still be around when I get home again in September. If only I could get rid of Robert during the school year, I'd have it made. It's a shame the kid doesn't go to boarding school.

Boarding school? Wait a minute. Yeah! That just might be the answer. Boarding school would be perfect!

All it would take would be a little planning. I could do it this summer. I know I could. Just one step at a time.

Let's see now. Where did I put my secret notebook?

# BARBARA PARK

was born and raised in Mount Holly, New Jersey. A graduate of the University of Alabama, she holds a B.S. in education. Barbara and her husband, Richard, now live in Phoenix, Arizona, with their two sons, Steven and David.

*Operation: Dump the Chump* is Barbara Park's second book. Her first novel, *Don't Make Me Smile,* was also published by Knopf.